Super Coco

Will You Be My Friend?

Written by Dr. Jay and Julie Lipoff
Illustrated by Ellisa DiRenzo

For more information on Super Coco "Will you be my friend?" visit Super Coco on Facebook, @supercocobook on Instagram and Twitter. To order books, visit Amazon.com or send a message to Dr. Jay Lipoff through Facebook, Instant Messenger or to drjchiro@hotmail.com, regarding special requests.

ISBN-13: 9781097105410

Dedication

This book is dedicated to our boys, Matthew and Lamden, who give us purpose and remind us that there is no gift greater than spending time together as a family. May the memories we foster remind them to take adventures, learn new things, appreciate the beauty in front of them while leaving their technology behind and no matter what, keep an open heart.

- Jay and Julie

To Eli and Anna, compassionate and courageous individuals who lived with Coco's artwork on their dining room table for a year without complaint.

- Ellisa

Acknowledgements

Special thanks go to our family and friends who help make life's adventure exciting and fun.

- Jay and Julie

Foreword

Although this story might be perceived as far-fetched, nature shows us repeatedly that the most unlikely bonds of friendships are formed by animals. While on family vacation in Aruba my wife noticed a black rooster and a pigeon spending time together near the big, red anchor in Seroe Colorado. Day after day we watched the pair as they seemed to stay close to a resident's drink cart that contained coconut water and had the words "Super Coco" written on its side.

The unlikely two were given names and the story was born. Julie and I wrote "Super Coco" to remind children to learn from adversity, embrace differences and always allow room for new friendships.

All of the animals in the story are native to Aruba but their names were changed to protect their identity. Like many islands, Aruba has a problem with stray dogs and cats, as well as needing sanctuaries for larger animals that are displaced or injured. In fact, many of the animals described in the book are real, like Cisco, the stray cat with his dark mohawk and tail. He hung out at our hotel at night and was very intimidating, but also extremely hungry. So a portion of the proceeds from the sales of this book will be donated to help find homes for needy animals and help others recover enough to survive on their own. Maybe they too can then set out across this beautiful island to build new friendships, like Coco.

Super Coco

Will You Be My Friend?

Written by Dr. Jay and Julie Lipoff

Illustrated by Ellisa DiRenzo

Sand
Dunes

California
Lighthouse

Wish Rock
Garden

Caribbean Sea

Alto Vista
Chapel

Arikok
National
Park

Bushiribana
Goldmine Ruins

Eagle Beach

Casibari Rock
Formation

Natural Pool

Ayo Rock
Formation

Dos Playa

Oranjestad

Guadirikiri Caves

Spanish
Lagoon

Mount
Jamanota

ARUBA

San
Nicholas

Seroe
Colorado

Baby Beach

N

On one happy island called Aruba, off the coast of South America, there lived a beautiful, but lonely, black rooster named Coco.

When Coco was small he became lost in a terrible storm that separated him from his family. He grew up alone in the Arikok National Park.

He enjoyed the warm weather and the scenery around him but what he wished for most was family and friends.

He knew it would be nice to have someone to do all the things that friends do together. He didn't know exactly where he was going to go but he decided to just start walking and this is how his adventure began.

One day he decided to explore other regions of the island to try to make some friends. *"How hard could it be?"* he thought to himself.

As he headed toward the biggest mountain on the island, the first animals he came across on his journey were wild goats. Most of the herd was grazing on thorny bushes and grasses but the kids were practicing jumping and challenging each other's strength. Coco asked them all, *"Will you be my friend?"*

George the goat came over, and in between chewing, replied, *"Sorry, we only hang with our own kind but good luck."* So Coco moved on.

Still enthusiastic to make friends Coco continued on his expedition and soon came across some whiptail lizards wiggling out of very interesting looking tonalite boulders.

One lizard had lost its tail. While some were speckled with brilliant blue, green and even white circles.

Coco politely approached and asked, *"Will you be my friend?"*

Lenny and Laura the lizards stepped closer and replied, *"Well you don't have any spots like we do and you aren't very colorful. How would you fit in?"*

Ayo Rock Formation

The sunshine was bright and warm. The air was windy but remained filled with hope as Coco pressed on. He followed a dirt path for hours that looked like it was leading up to whirling dinosaurs. He was a little scared but as he reached the top of the hill he veered to the right.

San Nicholas

As he entered an old town, he noticed some brilliant orange and white birds nesting high in a palm tree above him. *"Hello,"* Coco shouted.

"Can I help you?" asked Tucker the troupial bird.

"I'm Coco. I was just wondering will you be my friend?" Coco asked.

"I don't know how considering we are much prettier than you. Sorry Charlie," Tucker commented.

"My name is actually Coco," he said with some disappointment in his voice.

EDUCATION IS THE KEY TO **SUCCESS**

As he walked more and more miles he realized that the shore must be close because he could taste the salt in the air and hear the waves crashing against the coast. It was here that he noticed a drove of donkeys grazing on some grasses.

He bravely asked them, *"Is it okay if I stop and eat and will you be my friend?"* Desmond the donkey brushed some flies from his eyes with his tail and chuckled. *"We are so much bigger than you are. You should keep moving so you don't get hurt."* Coco ate quickly and moved on.

Coco surely wasn't going to let these animals discourage him. He kept walking and as he came to the beach he noticed a group of black-headed seagulls resting while facing the wind.

"How's it going?" he said. There was no response. Coco repeated himself, *"I say, how's it going?"*

Serena the seagull chirped, *"Well, I was sleeping."*

"I'm sorry," Coco explained, *"I was just curious,"* he hesitated, *"Will you be my friend?"*

"You can't fly" Serena replied abruptly, *"You wouldn't be able to keep up with us."*

The sand, sun and heat were taking its toll on Coco so he decided to move away from the beach. After some time walking, he saw some calm waters ahead and thought he would cool himself in the water.

Then he noticed some land crabs walking sideways along the edge of the lagoon.

As he cautiously moved closer he heard Carlos the crab yell, "*Ami no ta papia puítu,*" while waving his claws in the air from side to side.

"*My name is Coco and I was wondering, will you be my friend?*" he asked.

Carlos was harsh in his tone and said in broken words, "*I do not speak chicken.*" Coco thought laughter and smiling was communication enough but respected Carlos' words and continued on his way.

By now the sun was sinking lower in the sky and the leatherback sea turtles were coming up to nest on shore. Coco thought the turtles seemed slow and big.

"Miss would you mind," he paused briefly, *"Will you be my friend?"* he inquired shyly.

Tiana the turtle was just starting to lay her eggs in the sand near a Divi Divi tree when she replied, *"Son, you can't swim and you're so young honey. You need to find someone who enjoys doing the things you like to do."*

Coco wished he could find a friend just like that. As some baby turtles hatched and started to make their way to the sea, he waved goodbye and left the beach to head toward home.

This was not the way his friend quest was supposed to go. He decided to call it a day and take a rest in a nearby cave. Inside were lots of fruit bats that were just waking up.

Coco looked up and asked, *"Will you be my friend? We could go to sleep now and go have fun tomorrow!"*

Guadirikiri Caves

Benny the bat spoke up, *"If you can't stay awake all night like us we would never see each other. You should stay for now, but try searching in town tomorrow morning. You may have better luck there."*

Coco agreed and thanked him for his kindness.

The next day, Coco headed to a town he had seen the previous day, with renewed excitement. He saw a pack of stray dogs wandering towards people and weaving through traffic. He walked over and said, *"Hello"* to them.

An Arubian Cunucu dog responded, *"Hey."*

"Will you be my friend? We could go do something fun together?" Coco wondered.

"What's in it for us?" said Derrick.

"What do you have in mind?" inquired Dana.

"Kick a ball? Watch the clouds? Explore?" suggested Coco.

"No thanks. We do four-legged things, you wouldn't understand," they both replied.

Mile after mile, Coco searched and searched for a friendly face. As he approached a small building across the island he soon found himself surrounded by several feral cats.

Cisco was a very intimidating and unusual looking cat with a dark Mohawk and tail. He looked at Coco and asked, *"What are you doing in these parts chicken?"*

Nervously Coco mentioned he was trying to make some new friends and then bravely asked, *"Will you be my friend?"*

"We climb trees and prowl at night. I don't think you would fit in," Cisco fired back. Coco took his advice and quickly moved on.

As Coco walked away he noticed a bare-eyed pigeon off in the distance and all alone near the shore. He approached thoughtfully and reached out his wing in a friendly gesture. *"Hi. My name is Coco. How are you doing?"* he asked.

"Better now, thanks to you. My name is Patches and it is nice to meet you," she said.

"*I'm trying to stack these rocks and make a wish with each one, but with this wind I sure could use some help. Will you help me?*" she asked shyly.

"*Yes of course!*" Coco blurted out enthusiastically.

Patches told Coco that she was born with a damaged wing and some others in her flock picked on her because she looked different. This made her very sad so she set off on her own.

Casibari Rock Formation, Natural Pool, Bushiribana Goldmine Ruins

Coco and Patches seemed to really hit it off. They started spending their days doing many fun things together.

Some days they could be seen playing hide and seek,

splashing in the water pools and exploring castles.

Dos Playa, California Lighthouse, Sand Dunes

On other occasions they would be
kicking a ball on the beach,

counting stars by the lighthouse

and exploring the island
together.

The two were having so much fun laughing and playing together that it was impossible to ignore. The other animals on the island started to take notice.

They felt badly as they realized they had missed an opportunity to be friends with Coco because they couldn't see past their differences. One by one the animals started talking and came up with a plan they hoped would help make up for their mistakes. With any luck they would get another chance to play with the two coolest birds on the island.

So when the moment was right, all together they asked Coco and Patches, *"Will you be OUR friend?"*

Without any reservations, Coco, along with Patches, happily welcomed them all as friends. They had no problem accepting everyone no matter their differences. In fact, they loved having friends with unique appearances, interesting habits and more. It made them feel like a big, blended, happy family.

Word spread across the island of what an amazing friend Coco was and soon he became known as Super Coco.

Many years have passed but if you know where to look on the island you might just see Super Coco and Patches playing together because they are still the best of friends.

The End

After the completion of "Super Coco - Will You Be My Friend?" we returned to Aruba, specifically to the Big Red Anchor in Seroe Colorado, where the story began. We brought a copy of our book to Alipio, a local vendor who operates a cart filled with cold, fresh coconut water and delicious desserts with the words "Super Coco" written on its side.

Although we suffered a bit of a language barrier it was clear that Alipio understood that our brave, little rooster was named so because of his cart. He threw his hands up in the air and shouted enthusiastically, "SUPER COCO!" It was here that we solidified a genuine and true new friend.

Aruba is filled with a wonderful diversity of people and cultures, endless activities and adventures, and of course, new friendships waiting to be made. Go and experience "One Happy Island" and be sure to take a day to enjoy the charm of individual vendors and artisans who depend deeply on tourism. They will enrich your experience in a way that truly represents everything that makes Aruba so beautifully unique.

Made in the USA
Middletown, DE
15 July 2019